The Unforgiving Minute
Quantum Physics can be Murder

A Science-Fiction Thriller
by
Paul Casselle

Written & compiled with Scrivener

*First published on Amazon Kindle May 2017
(Version 101.3P – Print edition)*

ISBN: 978-1546646679

The Bit in the Middle Publishing

Disclaimer

This book is a work of fiction. The accuracy of any scientific ideas presented in this publication must not be construed as science fact. All characters depicted in this book are fictitious and any resemblance to persons living or dead is purely coincidental.

Copyright

Paul Casselle has asserted his right under the Copyright, Designs and Patents Act 1988 to be identified as the author of this work. This book may not be distributed in any format or digital medium without the written permission of the author.

paul@paulcasselle.com

© Paul Casselle 2017

Dedication

Thank you! - You know who you are.

If you can fill the unforgiving minute,
With sixty seconds' worth of distance run,
Yours is the Earth and everything that's in it,
And—which is more—you'll be a Man, my son!

If *(extract)*
Rudyard Kipling (1865-1936)

Part One

"Before you stick your finger in there, we need to talk."

Professor Edward Phillips looked up at his research assistant Alan Newton.

"Talk about what?" he asked evasively.

Alan gave Phillips a sour smile.

"We shouldn't be doing this, you know that."

The Professor looked down at a small black box resting in his lap. In the left-hand top corner, a single red LED glowed like a precious jewel.

"We have no idea what will happen," continued Alan.

"Yes we do," countered Phillips.

"No we don't," Alan turned his gaze away from his employer and mentor.

Phillips stroked the box, as if it were a beloved pet.

"It'll either work or it won't," said Phillips nodding his head. "It's a very sound theory."

The Professor looked around the sitting-room as if searching for support. Towering stacks of papers covered most surfaces. A number of piles had toppled and lay unresurrected, gathering dust. The room and

Paul Casselle

Phillips mirrored each other well; shabby and neglected. Under one of the tables was the only inanimate object that was free from a film of dust; a large blue suitcase.

The professor turned his attention back to his research assistant. He could not understand the young man's disquiet. After all, it was Alan who had done most of the calculations. In fact, it was his thesis that started the whole thing off; *A dangerous concept: The Many-Worlds Hypothesis & Quantum Suicide*.

"But that's it, Professor," Alan watched Phillips as he continued his visual tour of the room. "It is a very sound theory, but it is *just* a theory."

The Professor brought his attention back to the black box in his lap. He gently lifted it into the air.

"This looks pretty tangible to me," Phillips said mockingly.

Alan could now clearly see a hole in the side of the device. The grey-haired professor slowly circled his finger around the perimeter of the aperture with the delicacy and quiet excitement of performing an act of sexual stimulus.

Alan exhaled nervously.

"Please, I'm begging you. Just wait until we understand… until we know what we're doing."

Phillips stood up and walked a few paces. He put the box on a table. As he spoke Alan listened, but did not take his eyes from the device.

"Look," Phillips pontificated, as if giving a lecture, "the quantum theory of multiple universes is understood, mathematically. All we are doing is taking it to the next level; using a quantum event to cause a divergence of histories. If we can make this work, we will have done more than anyone before us. An infinity of multiverses will no longer be identical."

"... and they can never be rejoined; they will be totally different forever." Alan paused and swallowed hard. "We are messing with the fabric of space and time. We have no way of knowing what damage we may be doing."

"And that's you theorists all over, isn't it?" said Phillips, his tone uncharacteristically harsh. "You do your calculations and theoretical modelling, but when it comes to getting your hands dirty you squeal like a stuck pig."

"That's not fair," said Alan, his voice rising in pitch and volume. "I'm fearless when it comes to taking the universe apart, but that can be done without reckless experimentation. A theory can be revised, a physical catastrophe can't."

"Without proof, a theory is little more than an initial hypothesis," the Professor argued. "A starting point; the rantings of a madman. We need irrefutable, empirical proof."

Alan shook his head.

"Didn't Einstein say, 'God doesn't play dice with the universe'? What makes you think *you* can?"

"I'm not playing dice. I'm not gambling," said the Professor calmly. This universe of ours is totally knowable, Alan; there's no mystery. Everything is deterministic; cause and effect, cause and effect. If you know the cause, you can predict with one hundred percent certainty what the outcome will be."

"But… but…" Alan stammered, "that's the problem. Even if that were true, the world is too complex for us to calculate the possible effects of *every* interacting cause."

"But it *is* possible. Even if we find it nearly impossible to do."

"No Professor," Alan retorted, "the universe only seems deterministic from our perspective. At its core it is fundamentally random. And it's a reckless hubristic man that thinks he knows more than… more than…" he pointed vaguely towards the heavens, but said no more.

Alan's impassioned speech catapulted a memory into the Professor's mind and, before he realised it, he was speaking.

"You're as weak as my wife," said the Professor in a wistful voice.

An awkward silence fell on the argument.

"You've… you've… never spoken about your wife before."

Phillips' eyes were distant.

"She's dead," he said stoically.

"Yes, I know." Alan replied nodding. "Nobody in the department talks about her."

"And what does that tell you?" said Phillips, harshness returning to his tone.

"I… just wondered what happened… Why do you think I'm like her?"

The older man stared at his researcher for some time.

"Okay," he said finally, "like you, she believed the universe should be left alone. That we have no right to

The Unforgiving Minute

interfere with it. She would argue that because we live in the Middle world; much bigger than atoms and much smaller than the universe, we can only see the tiniest part of the whole. We can speculate, but must not touch."

"Well, I agree with that in principle," interjected Alan confidently.

"Well, I don't," Phillips said angrily. "What she totally missed is that unlike primitive human society, *now* we can see into the vastness of the heavens and deep into the infinitesimally small quantum world. We're no longer hampered by our physical limits because we now have incredibly sophisticated technologies. Just like you, she practiced a non-interventionist policy. But you two do differ in one fundamental aspect. You put your trust in physical laws, she put hers in something far less sound."

Alan furrowed his brow questioningly.

"God," said the Professor simply.

"Oh, she was religious?"

"A Jehovah's Witness!"

"That must have been fun!" said Alan, seeing more levity in religion than Phillips allowed himself to.

"No, not really. She died of cancer because she wouldn't let medical science intervene. She believed God…" Phillips' voice snared on emotion, "… would be there for her."

"I'm sorry."

"Don't be," said the Professor pulling himself back from the brink of anger. "It's not your fault." Phillips shook his head in small staccato movements. He looked reproachfully at his assistant. "Actually it is."

"What?" Alan looked stunned.

"It's people like you and her that fill the world with theoretical ideas, but you'd still be writing your notes on clay tablets if it weren't for people like me; people who have the balls to say it's down to us, God isn't coming."

"But that's reckless, Professor, when you have no idea what the repercussions will be."

Phillips looked at Alan with a wry smile.

"That may be true. It may be impossible for us to calculate everything and so predict the repercussions…" His smile broadened and he ran his tongue over his lips. "So, there's only one way to find out."

He moved quickly to the table, picked up the small black device and thrust his finger into the aperture. This action caused the release of a single electron within the box. A detector measured the spin of the particle; spin-up or spin-down, and from the binary outcome, an action was triggered. There was a second's pause; enough time for Alan's expression to turn to horror and Phillips' to fear. The machine produced a subtle click and Phillips screamed in shock.

Part Two

The Professor pulled his finger from the device. A bead of blood balanced on the end where the box had pricked him with a fine needle.

Alan looked at him, "Well?"

"Nothing," said Phillips, "except this."

He held up his blooded finger, then put it to his mouth; sucking the redness from it.

With his finger still between his lips, distorting his speech, Phillips continued.

"Did anything happen here?"

Alan shook his head.

"No, just your pathetic scream," Alan said sarcastically.

"So that means that if nothing happened to me, something did happen to all the other 'me's in fifty percent of the universes, right?"

"But we don't know what," countered Alan.

Excitedly Phillips started thumbing through the papers on his desk. Clouds of dust drifted across the room.

Paul Casselle

"The theory is quite clear as to what should happen," Phillips said without looking up. A drop of blood splashed onto the desk and Phillips returned his finger to his mouth. "The other fifty percent must have time-travelled."

Phillips had hoped it would be *his* fifty percent, but that was the thing that was nearly impossible to predict; in which half of the universes the subject would time-travel and in which half he would not.

"Alan, I may not have travelled, but it did work. My god, we've just split an infinity of identical universes into two sets of totally different ones."

"You can't be sure."

"Alan, look at me."

The young man looked up. His blond hair a little dishevelled and his clear eyes wet to overflowing.

"Alan - there are an infinity of 'me's out there who have just invented time-travel."

Alan rushed forward and grabbed the box.

"I can't take any more of this," he shouted moving quickly towards the door.

"What the hell are you doing, Alan? Give that back."

"No, we've done enough damage. Actually, we have no idea how much damage we've done. My god, Professor, you've got to stop."

Phillips stealthily approached and took hold of the box. The two men fought to get possession, but neither would give in. Out of the corner of his eye Phillips noticed Alan's left hand beginning to slide a little. The older man violently twisted the machine. Alan's hands were ripped away from the device leaving his pulling energy nowhere to go but to send him flying backwards.

It was all over. Phillips had the device, and Alan lay unconscious on the floor.

Part Three

His flesh melted from his skeleton and fell in heavy, liquid lumps to the floor. At least that was Phillips' perception of the current situation. His five senses; sight, taste, touch, smell and hearing, were all completely non-functional, and yet, in the total darkness of a terrifying moment, something inside his head was sure his flesh was sliding from his bones; but there was no pain. Phillips made a mental note; *no pain was observed during the time-passage.* Then in a flash of light, which he had no idea how to describe for his journal, he was sitting comfortably in the winged armchair, next to the fireplace, in his own sitting-room. He immediately looked up to share everything with Alan, but Alan was not there.

    He felt a little stunned that something, rather than nothing, had happened. He looked up at the clock on the wall; ten past ten. For the very first time, a man had travelled three hours into the future.

    The small black box snuggled in his lap. A green LED flashed slowly indicating recent activation of the device. Phillips always thought of it as The Device. He

The Unforgiving Minute

didn't have the gall to call it after its actual function. 'Time Machine', seemed just too ridiculous. Device would do for now; even if now had become a less certain term than it had been three hours before…

Sitting in his armchair, a month later, an irreducible question, poked at his scientific brain, So what did all this mean? You spend your life working to create something new, something startlingly new, like cold fusion or manned-flight or turning lead into gold, but what then? Phillips believed that great scientific discoveries and inventions are either used for earth-shattering paradigm shifts or comically banal hedonism. Humanity tends to act with either god-like majesty or churlish depravity; rarely anything in between. He had not let his species down. Since the first successful time-passage he had been playing with The Device like a kitten with a ball of wool. Mostly, he had been using it to side-step any situation he didn't want to endure. Three weeks ago he had avoided a boring student debate by time-passaging to the following morning. Last week he time-passaged from waking up to having lunch at the university, completely missing having to give the inaugural first years' lecture. And just yesterday he had avoided an embarrassing prostate examination by jumping to the moment after his GP's surgical gloves had been removed.

He had spent his life working at universities, and every break-though and invention in which he had been instrumental had been stolen by the various academies. The Device had been his own work in his own time. This

Paul Casselle

was his and no-one was going to take it from him. When he felt the time was right, and he was satisfied with his results, he would announce his astonishing invention to the world. Until then he was going to enjoy himself as he so often wanted to and so rarely did. Just now Phillips was having the time of his life; literally.

The one thing that kept troubling him was the strange disappearance of Alan. He hadn't even left a note; his mobile phone just went to voicemail and no-one at the university had seen him for weeks.

It was three o'clock in the afternoon, and Phillips was at home. As it was Friday, he had finished his university duties for the week and was looking forward to writing up further notes on The Device. The phone rang. It was the Dean.

"Hello, Phillips?"

The Dean, who always claimed superiority by calling everyone by their surname like a public school headmaster, had an unmistakable voice. An anachronistic cross between Prince Charles and Margaret Thatcher.

"Yes, Dean."

"Are you busy?"

"Not particularly, but it really depends what you are going to ask of me."

"Come now, Phillips. You act as if I always ask something of you."

"You do."

"Do I? Does it get me anywhere?"

"Rarely, but you're welcome to give it a go."

The Unforgiving Minute

"Okay. Drinks, Phillips. I need you to come for drinks."

"When?"

"Tonight, old boy. Party from the University of Tokyo. They're insisting on meeting our Professor of Particle Physics."

"Japanese insisting!?"

"Well, more requesting; inscrutably."

There was silence on both ends of the line.

"You will come, won't you, Phillips? Take one for the team and all that."

"I promise to do my professional duty."

"Good. See you later old man. Drinks at eight."

The line went dead.

Phillips smiled to himself as he got The Device ready. He flicked the on/off switch and the red LED glowed. Then, after checking the exact time on the wall clock, he set the next day's date and the current time, plus five minutes, on the display on the top of the device.

Checking the clock again he noted he now had three minutes left. He sat in his armchair and turned the device in his hands exposing the finger sized aperture. He watched the clock count down the seconds to the time he had set on the machine's display. At that exact time, he thrust his finger into the aperture and closed his eyes.

He stayed like this for the next few seconds before lifting his eyelids. He found he was still in the armchair, but that didn't mean anything bad; he often returned to the armchair after a jump. The LED had changed from

Paul Casselle

steady red to flashing green. That simply meant the machine had activated; the outcome was still not certain. What had just occurred could be one of two scenarios. A, he had jumped to the following day or; B, nothing had happened. The only way to tell was to check the date on his computer or some other device. If it was the next day, he had successfully jumped, if not, then he would have to go for drinks, and tomorrow, at this exact time, an even stranger thing would happen. He opened his laptop. The date had not changed. Drinks then, he thought, and *amuse-bouches* with chopsticks.

Part Four

Phillips awoke in his favourite winged armchair. The Dean's drinks party had gone on until late. He had found the Japanese rather good fun, and had enjoyed discussing various advances in quantum physics, and shooting down their ludicrous belief that Chaos theory exposed a non-deterministic universe. Just because we cannot understand something doesn't mean we should jump to fantastic explanations. Everything is knowable. It's simply a question of fearless research and having the balls to go through with experimentation. The truth, when we finally understand it, is always awe-inspiring enough. For Phillips, a belief that the future is fundamentally unknowable; a belief in randomness; effects without a cause, was as crazy as a belief in God.

The phone rang. It was the Dean.

"Phillips, where the hell were you last night? I kept making excuses to my guests, but you didn't arrive and wouldn't answer your phone."

After a hesitant pause Phillips responded.

15

"Dean, I'm so sorry. I wasn't feeling well and sat down for a minute, but didn't wake up until this morning. I'm so, so sorry."

The line went dead.

It had happened again; this strange memory aberration that came with each use of The Device. Over the past few weeks Phillips had thought of hundreds of possible theories to explain the anomaly, but none were compelling. In one instance, he would jump a period of time and on returning, hear reports of what he did while he was jumping, but he would have no memory of the period. However, on occasions, like last night, the jump would not work. He would go through the event he was trying to avoid, but find that although he had full recollection of the events he had just lived through, everyone involved had no memory of him being present at all.

Phillips wearily pulled himself out of the comfort of the chair and walked towards his desk; another day of trying to make sense of this. There was a knock at the door. He sighed and closed his eyes. The knock came again, but louder and more insistent. Phillips went to the door and opened it. Two men in badly fitting suits were revealed. The one in the most creased suit spoke.

"Professor Phillips?"

"Yes."

"Professor Edward Vivian Phillips?"

"Still yes," he said with a playful smile.

"Professor Phillips, I'm arresting you for the murder of Alan Newton."

Part Five

Judge Hughes appeared at the panelled oak door and moved quickly to his chair. The court rose with Pavlovian reverence. The Judge sat down and the court followed his lead. Two people were left standing; the clerk of the court and Phillips, mournfully alone in the dock.

"You are Edward Vivian Phillips?"

"Yes," said Phillips, with the energy of a dying man.

"Edward Vivian Phillips, you are charged that on the third day of September two thousand and twenty-nine you did wilfully murder Alan Newton and subsequently did bury his body in Bromarsh woods." The clerk paused and looked up from the charge sheet to meet Phillips' gaze. "How do you plead; guilty or not guilty?"

Phillips squeezed his eyes shut hoping that, when he opened them, he would find himself in his winged armchair; waking from a nightmare. His eyes blinked open.

"Not guilty."

The newspaper reporters mumbled excitedly in the gallery and settled in for the theatrics of a juicy murder trial.

"Order, order," boomed Judge Hughes, reminding the court both of his presence and supremacy. "Mr Premburton? Please call your first witness."

The council for the Crown stood up and bowed ingratiatingly towards the bench.

"I call Joseph Nestor."

A man in his early thirties entered the court and took the witness stand. The clerk approached him carrying a selection of religious tomes. Scanning through the leather-bound selection in his hands, the clerk spoke without looking up.

"Religion?"

"No, thanks. I'm trying to give them up," joked Nestor.

Judge Hughes shot a disapproving glance at the young man.

"Sorry. I'm not religious."

The clerk continued, unfazed, and with great pomp and circumstance.

"Raise your right hand and read the words on the card."

"I swear to give the truth, the whole truth and nothing but the truth."

Premburton rose to his feet as the clerk returned to his desk.

"Mr Nestor, you are the neighbour of Professor Phillips?"

"Yes, I live in the house next to his."

The Unforgiving Minute

"In fact, they are semi-detached, are they not?"

"Yes, they are."

"I understand they are quite new buildings."

"Built in two thousand and twenty-five. Me and the Professor were the first people to live in them."

"So, they'll be those new graphene-frame affairs with ultra-thin walls, right?"

"Yeah, that's right, ultra-thin walls. I can't even have bare floorboards because they'd make too much noise. I know the Professor needs to concentrate on his work. You know what I mean?"

Yes, I know exactly what you mean. So, you must hear various noises from the Professor's house."

"Sometimes, yeah."

"Mr Nestor, were you at home on the evening of the third of September this year?"

"Yes, I was."

"And did you hear anything unusual through those ultra-thin walls of yours?"

Smythe, counsel for the defence, shot to his feet.

"M'lud, 'anything unusual' calls for subjective speculation."

The judge scratched his chin.

"Get to the point quickly, Mr Premburton."

Nestor looked towards the Professor.

"Please look at me, Mr Nestor," said Premburton with quiet insistence. "Did you hear anything… you would not usually expect to hear?"

"Yes."

"What did you hear?"

"Raised voices."

"Can you tell us exactly what you heard?'

"Well, at first it was just the usual talking; the Professor and Alan."

"Would that be Alan Newton?"

"Yes."

"How can you be sure it was Alan Newton with the Professor?"

"I'd seen him arrive earlier. I was looking out of the front window." Nestor shot a guilty look at the Judge. "I wasn't spying or anything like that."

"No one's accusing you of anything, Mr Nestor," said Premburton. "Please continue with what happened next."

"Well, their voices started to get louder. Bit of a barney, I thought, but then it went quiet for a minute, and then there was a crash, like something heavy falling on the floor. And that was it."

"What time was this?"

"Nine o'clock."

"How can you be so accurate?"

"Holby City."

"I'm sorry… Holby City?"

"The TV programme. It had just finished… Nine o'clock."

"Indeed. Did anything else happen?"

"Yes. A few minutes later I heard the Professor's front door bang. So, I looked out of the window and saw the Professor carrying something heavy to his car."

"How do you know it was heavy?"

"Well, it was a big black plastic thing and he was half carrying it, half dragging it." A slight smile pulled

The Unforgiving Minute

at Nestor's mouth. "I remember I thought, my god, the Professor's done him in."

"Done him in?"

"Yeah, you know… Well, anyway, that's all I saw."

"Thank you Mr Nestor," Premburton turned to Mr Smythe, "Your witness."

Smythe stood slowly.

"Mr Nestor, I only have a few questions for you."

Smythe gave Nestor a wide disarming smile.

"You are sure it was Professor Phillips that you saw half dragging, half carrying something to his car?"

"Yes."

"And you are certain he came out of his house; the Professor's house?"

"Yes."

Smythe held up a photograph, "Please enter this as Defence Exhibit One."

He gave the photograph to an usher who, in turn, passed it to Nestor.

"Do you recognise this view, Mr Nestor?"

"Yeah, it's the view from my front window."

"Can you see the Professor's front door in that photograph?"

"Well, no. Not from that angle."

Smythe stared at the witness for a few seconds.

"No, not from that angle. How about the road, can you see that?"

"Yeah, through the branches of the tree."

"Through the branches of the tree," Smythe repeated slowly. "That is a very tall and wide tree. How was it possible to see so clearly with it obscuring your view?"

"It's autumn," said Nestor incredulously, "all the leaves have dropped off."

"Indeed," Smythe said nodding his head. "All the leaves had dropped off. Do you know what sort of tree that is, Mr Nestor?"

"No."

"It's a conifer… with dense foliage; an evergreen. The leaves don't 'drop off' even in autumn. Mr Nestor, the truth is that because of that tree you cannot see the Professor's front door at any angle, and even though this picture was taken in broad daylight, rather than at nine o'clock on a September evening, you can barely see the road. So, I ask you again, Mr Nestor. Are you sure you saw the professor?"

"Well, not one hundred percent, no, but I heard his door shut so it must have been him."

Smythe interlocked the fingers of his hands and flexed them thoughtfully.

"Okay, let us recap what you know for sure. You believe someone arrived at the Professor's house. We have established you could not see from your window, so you can't be sure who it was or if there was a visitor at all. You heard raised voices through the wall, which could have been a radio or television…"

"No, I know what I saw…"

"Please let me finish, Mr Nestor," Smythe insisted.

Judge Hughes cleared his throat.

"Mr Nestor…"

Nestor mumbled under his breath.

The Unforgiving Minute

"… to continue," Smythe seamlessly resumed, "you then heard something crash to the floor. A most unusual thing to happen. There is no way that could be anything but sinister?"

"M'lud," shouted Premburton, losing his poise for the first time in the proceedings.

"Mr Smythe," intoned the judge, heavily, "you have, as have the witnesses, a duty to stick to the facts, rather than assumptive polemics. Please do so."

"M'lud," said Smythe, bowing his head to the Judge, then turning back to the witness "you then hear, but cannot see, a door slam closed. And then see something in the darkness, through the thick foliage of a large tree, that you take to be Professor Phillips dragging something large to his car. Do I have that right?"

"Well that was definitely a body he was dragging."

"But you couldn't see it, could you?"

Nestor transferred his weight from one leg to the other.

"No, but that *thump, thump, thump* down the stairs, had to be a body."

"You couldn't be mistaken?"

"I know what I heard."

"Okay, Mr Nestor."

Smythe signalled his assistant. The young woman touched the play button on an audio/visual panel set into the desk. A distinct, rhythmic *thump, thump, thump* was heard.

"Is that like the sound you heard, Mr Nestor?"

"Yes, that's it exactly!"

Smythe signalled his assistant again. This time a large flat-panel screen flickered on. The same sound, thump, thump, thump, came over the audio, but on the screen was Smythe pulling a large blue wheelie suitcase down the steps to the Professor's house; *thump, thump, thump*. When he reached the bottom, he turned to the camera.

"That's Professor Phillips' suitcase. On the night in question he went to Aldeburgh-on-Sea for a few days. No more questions, M'lud," said Smythe with practised understatement as he retook his seat.

The next witness was a tall, thin, academic man. His hands were striking; fine and balanced with long fingers, like those of a pianist or a surgeon.

After swearing in, the man stood erect and benign. But, he nevertheless looked like a gentleman whose patience should not be tested.

"Dr Greenspan, you are the forensic pathologist that conducted the autopsy on Alan Newton?" asked Premburton.

"Yes, I am," responded Greenspan with a steady voice that perfectly matched his appearance.

"Will you kindly tell us your findings?"

"Certainly. The deceased had been in a good state of health before his death. He had bruising to his forearms and his right hip. There was a deep wound, seven centimetres long, on his right temple. He also suffered considerable haemorrhaging to the front right quadrant of his brain."

"And the cause of death?"

"A massive cerebral haemorrhage."

The Unforgiving Minute

"I understand the body was found around eight o'clock on the second of October two thousand and twenty-nine, is that correct?"

"Yes, it is."

"Can you estimate the time of death?"

"Using standard biological markers, between twenty-eight and thirty-two days previously."

"Can you tell us how the body was found?"

"I'm sorry, no. I think it was someone walking their dog…"

"No, sorry Doctor. I meant was the body dumped in the bushes or…?"

"Oh, I see. No, the body had been buried."

Premburton's eyes widened and his mouth dropped open, as if auditioning the emotion of surprise for a pantomime producer.

"Buried? So whoever killed him obviously took their time?"

Smythe jumped to his feet.

"M'lud. The question calls for an opinion rather than factual evidence."

The Judge nodded his head sagely.

"Mr Premburton, I'd appreciate questions that are a little less rhetorical in nature, if you'd be so kind."

"M'lud. Doctor Greenspan, may I ask how long you have been a forensic pathologist?"

"This year will be thirty-five years."

"So, I think we can assume you have a wealth of experience?"

Greenspan turned his eyes downward and momentarily tilted his head to one side.

"In what cases do you find a victim buried rather than left above ground?"

"Generally when the perpetrator has more time; when they're not rushed."

"Or when they have pre-planned the burial?"

Smythe was on his feet before the end of the last syllable.

"M'lud," protested the defence lawyer.

"You have been warned, Mr Premburton. I will not warn you again," said Judge Hughes.

"I withdraw the question," said Premburton with unconvincing contrition.

Premburton sat down and Smythe rose from his chair.

"Dr Greenspan, you say the cause of death was a massive cerebral haemorrhage."

"Yes."

"And the haemorrhage was the result of the head trauma?"

"Without a doubt."

"Did you establish how the head wound was sustained?"

"Yes, blood and skin belonging to the deceased was found on the edge of a table at Professor Phillips' house. The edge of the table was, undoubtedly, the cause of the wound"

"What sort of table was that, at the Professor's house? For instance, was it a heavy table or one that could easily be picked up?"

The Unforgiving Minute

"M'lud," barked Premburton, half standing, "The question calls for an opinion outside of the witness's expertise."

"I quite agree, Mr Premburton," said the judge, "However, I do not think one needs a degree in furniture making to be able to say whether a table is light enough to be picked up or not. You may answer the question, Dr Greenspan."

"The table had a heavy wooden base and a thick glass top. In my opinion…" he paused, "… it would not be possible for a single person to lift it."

"So, there is no way the table could have been swung; as a weapon?"

"No, I believe not."

"And the bruising to the arms?"

"Consistent with a struggle."

"A violent struggle?"

"The bruising was very superficial. There is no indication of anything prolonged or particularly violent."

"And lastly," Smythe concluded, "Dr Greenspan, did you find any forensic evidence of Professor Phillips having been at Bromarsh Woods?"

Premburton shifted in his chair and chewed his lip.

"No. No soil or flora samples from the woods were found on any of Professor Phillips' shoes or clothes."

"So there is no evidence that the Professor was ever in Bromarsh Woods?"

"No, there is not."

"How probable is that? That a man who drags a body into the woods and digs a grave, would have no soil or flora on his clothes?"

"Highly improbable."

"Thank you doctor. No more questions," said Smythe retaking his seat.

Part Six

Phillips had had great faith in Smythe from the moment he had met him. He came highly recommended and had an excellent record of acquittals. After the performance Phillips had just witnessed, he was feeling strangely sanguine considering he was standing trial for murder. It seemed that there was no hard evidence that he had committed any crime. Only that somehow Alan had hit his head on Phillips' table, but there was very little to link the Professor to that and nothing to implicate him in any other part of Alan's demise.

The court was in recess, and Phillips was in a cell with Smythe.

"But what about the statement I gave to the police?" asked Phillips.

Smythe gave a slight shake of the head and shrugged.

"Rantings of a confused, innocent man. I'll simply say you were mistaken; it was all a momentary aberration."

Phillips shook his head more vigorously than his barrister.

"But that's not true. I'm not going to let you make things up. I have absolutely no idea how Alan ended up hitting his head or how he got from my house to Bromarsh Woods, but I do know exactly what happened to me."

"Look Professor, the only evidence that links you with Alan Newton's death is that he hit his head on your table. There is only circumstantial evidence that you were even there when that happened. And there is nothing to say you were ever in Bromarsh Woods. Just let me give an explanation to your police statement and we are pretty sure to get an acquittal."

Phillips was only half listening to his lawyer.

"What about Aldeburgh-on-Sea?" said Phillips.

"What about it?"

"You are claiming that what my neighbour heard was me wheeling my suitcase down my front steps, going on a trip to Aldeburgh-on-Sea."

"Yes, that's right," Smythe agreed.

"But no one at Aldeburgh-on-Sea remembers me being there. And more to the point nor do I."

"That still doesn't hurt your case, Professor," Smythe insisted. "They have nothing to link you to the death of Newton and no motive, only opportunity; that is not enough to secure a conviction. Therefore, the Judge will have to move to an acquittal."

"An acquittal that will lead to reports of me being a mad scientist. What I said in my statement is true."

"But it won't help your case. In fact, it will almost definitely lose it."

Phillips pushed his chair back and paced the cell.

The Unforgiving Minute

"Win the case and destroy my reputation?"

Smythe stayed quiet for a few seconds. A face appeared at the spy hatch on the door.

"Excuse me Mr Smythe, they're asking for you and the prisoner."

"Thank you Charlie, we're just finishing. Professor, please?"

"Mr Smythe, I am who I am; a scientist. And a scientist who is scared to face the truth, is a poor scientist indeed."

The court was back in session. Judge Hughes addressed the counsel for the prosecution.

"Mr Premburton, do you have further witnesses?"

Premburton rose to his feet languidly.

"No M'lud, the prosecution rests."

"Mr Smythe, will you be calling witnesses?"

Smythe, with the look of a cream-filled cat, stood, "No, M'lud."

The judge began to address the court, but was interrupted by a noise from the dock.

"Professor Phillips; you want to say something?"

Smythe looked to the heavens and let out a deflating sigh; almost a whimper.

"I wish to give evidence, your honour."

The judge addressed the defence counsel.

"Mr Smythe?"

"M'lud, I have instructed my client that he does not need to give evidence and I would urge him, in his best interests, that he sits down and allows your honour to continue."

"Professor Phillips," said Judge Hughes, "I was about to sum-up, and I can tell you that you would not have been disappointed with my conclusions. However, if you choose to give evidence, by your own volition, I must warn you that you may harm your own defence. So, are you sure you need to say whatever it is you have on your mind?"

"I am, your honour."

"Mr Smythe, your witness."

Smythe waited while Phillips was sworn in, then spoke.

"Professor Phillips, you are Professor of Particle Physics at Trinity College, Cambridge?

"I am."

"And how long have you held this position?"

"Twenty-six years."

"So it would be reasonable to say you are well-respected in your field?"

The merest smile coloured the Professor's face.

"You may say that. I couldn't possibly comment."

"Were you not the leader of the London ELHC?" Judge Hughes interrupted.

"ELHC?"

"The Extremely Large Hadron Collider, M'lud. A very advanced particle accelerator." Smythe turned back to Phillips. "Professor?"

"Yes, I had that honour."

"Am I also correct… Professor… in saying you have recently been involved with some award-winning advances in quantum physics?"

The Unforgiving Minute

"Yes, the multiverse and the use of this for time-tra..."

"Indeed, Professor," Smythe interrupted hastily. "Very interesting. Now, it is true, is it not, that science as advanced as your work can sometimes seem... how shall we put it... difficult for the average man to understand?

"I suppose so."

"Maybe even... sometimes seeming... a little unbelievable? Aren't pioneering scientists often lampooned for their advanced ideas?"

Judge Hughes leant forwards, "Mr Smythe, this is all very interesting, but might I trouble you to get back to the case?"

"M'lud, I am attempting to establish the credentials of Professor Phillips and the fact that some of his research may be beyond the understanding of the man in the street."

"Well, Mr Smythe, I believe you have achieved your aim most admirably. Please move on."

"M'lud. So, Professor, when you speak of your research into the possibility of... say... time-travel, this might be one of those 'hard to believe' projects?"

"I would go further..."

Smythe quickly cut him off, "A yes or no will suffice."

"Yes."

"So it may be considered foolish if someone, not conversant with extremely advanced physics, were to jump to conclusions about an eminent Professor's advanced theories?"

"I guess."

"No more questions, M'lud."

Premburton bowed his head to the Judge and turned to Phillips.

"Professor Phillips, did you know Alan Newton?"

"Yes, he was my research fellow."

"Were you friends?"

"No, not really friends. We just worked together."

"And what was that working relationship like? Did you get on?"

Phillips shifted a little.

"Yes, we got on just fine."

"You didn't argue?"

"Well everyone argues at times…"

"Simply yes or no, Professor Phillips. Did you and Alan Newton argue?"

"No."

Premburton could not stop an involuntary raising of one eyebrow.

"Are you sure, Professor Phillips?"

"Yes, Alan and I got on well."

"Okay, Professor, let's change tack a little. Where were you on the night in question?"

"At home."

"Were you alone?"

"No."

"Who was at your home with you?"

"Alan Newton."

"And what were you doing?"

"We were just chatting."

"Just chatting, Professor Phillips?"

The Unforgiving Minute

"Yes."

"All evening, Professor?"

"Yes, all evening."

"So, Alan Newton and you spent a whole evening, at your home, just chatting?"

"Yes."

"Unusual behaviour for two people who are just work colleagues and not friends. Professor Phillips, what time did Alan Newton leave your home?"

"I don't know."

"You don't know, Professor?" Premburton looked at the jury and repeated. "You don't know, Professor? And why is that? Did you fall asleep, were you called away? Please tell the jury why you don't remember?"

"Because I wasn't there when he left."

"So, Professor, where were you?"

"To be truthful, I don't know."

"Oh, come now, Professor, I think you do."

Premburton held up some papers. He smiled at Smythe, whose eyes just stared, helplessly.

"This is the statement you gave to the police. You seemed very clear about your whereabouts in here."

Phillips felt suddenly sick and weak. He may be committed to the truth, but that didn't make it easy.

"Would you like to tell us or shall I read from your statement. Professor Phillips?"

Phillips breathed in and sighed heavily.

"I wasn't there when Alan left because… because…"

"Yes, Professor, because?"

"… because I was time-travelling."

Part Seven

Phillips stared out between the iron bars of a small window. The cell was below ground level, and all he could see were the feet of passers-by. A few years of this, he thought, and he'd be an expert on footwear.

The grey-painted brick cell was just large enough for Smythe, Phillips and a table and two chairs. The room stank of despair, but the Professor detected another aroma; a sweet note of camphor coming from Smythe's barristers' gown. Liberty breeds complacent profligacy, but conversely, incarceration makes one a miser of the senses.

"So, what now, Mr Smythe?'

"Now Professor, you have backed us into a corner. I told you to leave it alone, but unfortunately I can only advise."

Phillips sat down making the sign of the cross.

"I absolve you, my son."

Smythe held his disapproving expression.

"The prosecution are willing to offer a deal."

"Really?"

The Unforgiving Minute

"As far as the charge of murder is concerned, there is no evidence of motive, and no compelling evidence of manslaughter. They could charge you with Perverting the Course of Justice; which carries a maximum sentence of life, but they are inclined against that as it is very rare to get a conviction."

"So, what are they offering?"

"Wasting Police Time. You'll get three years and be out in under two."

"Two years," said Phillips slowly, "What do I have to do?"

"You plead guilty to the lesser charge of Wasting Police Time, or they will send you for psychiatric assessment at Broadmoor and throw away the key."

"Not much of a choice."

Smythe's face flashed with anger.

"And whose fault is that?"

Phillips took a deep breath, and thought about two years of the dank smell of imprisonment, and two years of staring at shoes through cold iron bars.

"Can you bring me my machine?" asked the Professor.

The barrister smiled and gasped.

"Your machine?"

"Yes, the so called time machine."

"I know what machine you're talking about. I can't understand why you want it. Surely a decision about the deal on offer is a little more pressing just now?"

"As appealing as an indeterminate period in Broadmoor is, I think I'll go for pleading guilty to Wasting Police Time."

Paul Casselle

The sound of a key in the cell's door prompted the two men to rise.

"Will you get me my machine?"

"I'll see what I can do."

It was only twenty minutes before the Professor re-entered the cell as a convicted prisoner.

"You just wait here, sir," said the warder. "The van will come soon to take you to the prison."

They say that reality is rarely as bad as you imagine it to be. Without a doubt, this was the exception that proved the rule. Phillips' teeth were actually chattering, and his clothes were damp with sweat, even though he could see his breath in the cold air.

"Mr Smythe left something for you. It's on the table," said the warder.

The cell door clanged.

Phillips was comforted by seeing something familiar resting inoffensively on the table. The Device, even though it was the instrument of all this tragedy still appealed to his sense of cognitive ease. Sitting down, he pulled the machine towards himself. He stroked it affectionately, then adjusted the date on the device's display.

The machine made no noise as he flicked the switch to on. There was just the usual LED glow, casting a blood red hue across the grey walls. Phillips put his finger into the device and within seconds felt the prick of the needle. But that was all that happened. He was not transported to the end of his prison sentence. A key rattled in the door, and he hastily pushed his finger into

The Unforgiving Minute

the machine again. This time there was no sensation from the needle.

"If you'd come with me, Professor Phillips?" said the warder.

The Professor did not look up. He pulled his hand back to try the machine again, but a strong grip on his wrist prevented him from doing so. He gazed at the kindly face of the warder.

"It's Charlie, isn't it?"

"Yes, Sir, Charlie. If you could just put that thing on the table, we'll get you processed and on your way."

"It didn't work, Charlie."

"Yes, Sir."

"The one time I really needed it, it didn't work."

"Well let's not worry about that now... Come on, Sir... Best not keep the escort waiting."

Phillips stood, held in the firm hands of the warder.

"You're a good man, Charlie. Do you know that?"

"I do my best, Sir."

▽

Part Eight

Julie had been back in England for nearly six weeks. As she had been in Australia for the last two years, her memories of a cold climate had all but faded. As she climbed out of her car and walked from the carpark, she was reminded again, by a bitter gust of wind, that she had still not acclimatised to the northern hemisphere.

Her move to Australia had been motivated by a job offer that would have been career suicide to turn down, but it had meant a long separation from her husband. He had been very understanding, possibly because he worked in the same field, however, it had proved very difficult for both of them. On any other occasion, this impromptu return to England would have been a godsend for her marriage, but not this time.

This was an open prison, so security was no more than one would expect to find at the average local airport, and therefore not too tedious. She had arranged everything in advance which further speeded up the procedure, yet her internal nervousness conspired to make the process seem far too long and left her patience far too short.

Julie recognised Professor Phillips the moment he walked into the visitors' hall. The old man stood at the entrance and scanned the space apparently recognising no one. Julie waved to him, and Phillips moved towards her with trepidation. He stood tight-lipped next to the table at which she sat.

"I'm told that you claim to be a physicist," said Phillips.

Julie looked up at the Professor and nodded.

"I am. I've been working at Sydney University."

"Sydney?" echoed the Professor. "What's your name?"

"Julie, Julie Taggart."

"And what brings you back to England, Miss Taggart?" asked Phillips.

"A family bereavement."

"I'm sorry," said Phillips softening a little. "Why did you want to see me?"

"Won't you sit, Professor?" Julie said. "I'm getting a sore neck talking to you like this."

Phillips sat down, and looked hard into Julie's eyes.

"Are you a journalist?"

"No, I told you, I'm a physicist from Sydney University."

"I've had a lot of journalists trying to get an interview with me. Apparently, I'm a good story. So far, three of them have claimed to be physicists."

"Professor Phillips," Julie pleaded, "I'm not lying. I really am a physicist."

"Then a little test should be no problem."

Julie's insides churned and gurgled. She berated herself for being so naïve, that he would just take her at her word.

"What sort of test?"

Phillips sat back in his chair and narrowed his eyes.

"Okay, what is the Haber Bosch Process?"

Julie snorted lightly through her nose.

"It's a process to fix atmospheric nitrogen... but that's chemistry not physics."

"What's the Pauli exclusion principle?" continued the Professor.

"That two or more identical fermions cannot occupy the same quantum state."

"What's the Fourth Law of Thermodynamics?

"There *are* four Laws, but there isn't a fourth Law," Julie answered.

A glow was beginning to lighten the pallor of Phillips face as if asking these questions were transporting him back to the lecture theatre.

"That sounds like a contradiction," said Phillips.

"Well," Julie sighed, "there are Laws One, Two and Three, but the fourth Law isn't called the forth Law." Phillips stared at her with a poker face. "It's known as the Zeroth Law."

"Yeah," said Phillips dismissively, "this is all schoolboy stuff. How about something really difficult."

"Go ahead, Professor."

"Explain the Rodriguez maximum peak principle."

Julie narrowed her eyes and sat up in her chair.

"The what?"

The Unforgiving Minute

"If you are a physicist, there is no way you don't know the Rodriguez maximum peak principle. So, go ahead 'not-a-journalist'... explain."

Julie sat silently studying the prisoner opposite her. Phillips suddenly got up.

"Next time you want a story, young woman, do some research before you try to bluff."

The Professor turned and started to walk back towards the entrance.

"Professor?" Julie called out, "I am not a journalist." Phillips continued walking and did not turn around. "Professor, there *is* no Rodriguez maximum peak principle." Phillips stopped. "You just made it up!"

The professor turned slowly and gazed inscrutably at his young visitor.

"Lucky guess," he said finally, "but sorry, still no cigar," he turned to leave again.

"I came here, Professor to talk to you about the anomaly with your 'Device'."

Phillips stopped and turned back to Julie.

"What anomaly?"

"The memory anomaly, Professor," said Julie. "I think the memory effect is caused by quantum entanglement."

Part Nine

Every day after lunch, Phillips and the other prisoners were turfed out into the recreation hall for two and a half hours. Two sets of double doors opened off from the room onto the great outdoors where the inmates could go for short walks around the heavily-fenced grass areas.

Phillips invariably chose to stay inside and sit at a table with his notes and 'work'. He interacted with the other prisoners very little, and most of them seemed as wary of *him* as he was of *them*. Every two weeks he had a visit from Julie, where they would discuss The Device, and try to fully understand the physics behind its operation and how to accurately control it, but more than this they discussed its implications and what it would mean to mankind's future.

Phillips had been hyper-focussed on the mountains of papers in front of him for the last forty minutes. Although he had realised that he needed desperately to go to the toilet twenty minutes ago, he had not managed to tear himself away from the set of calculations he was currently trying to solve. He told himself time after time

The Unforgiving Minute

that when he completed the next equation with which he was grappling, he would take a moment and have a pee, but the toilet break had not happened. As he finished one calculation, the next begged for his attention with irresistible urgency, and his bladder was put on hold one more time.

A twinge in his groin took him by surprise. For a moment he thought he was going to wet himself right there in the recreation hall. He carefully placed his pencil onto the table, and breathed slowly, mentally trying to sooth his irate bladder. The crisis passed, and Phillips was well aware that only extreme good fortune had prevented him from an embarrassment he might never have survived. He rose carefully and headed with some urgency towards the lavatories.

Sitting on a toilet inside a cubicle, the long-repressed torrent finally exploded from him. It was an enormous relief, however, when gates have been forced to stay closed against an almost irresistible force for so long, hinges tend to become seized. Reanimation is often a painful affair.

For many years, Phillips had sat down to urinate. Somehow it felt more dignified than standing, and as the years diminished his physical abilities, he found it eminently more relaxing. But even as a fitter younger man, standing in front of a line of urinals had never appealed to him. Micturition for Phillips was as private an affair as defecation; a locked cubicle was the only civilised place for the act.

The Professor heard some people enter the toilet, but what piqued his interest was the furtive whispers in which they spoke. They obviously had failed to realise that someone may already be in the lavatory, secluded inside a cubicle, and so they went about their business as if in private. However, Phillips *was* there, within earshot, and he felt trapped. In prison the first rule you learn is to mind your own business. Curiosity was as unwelcome in gaol as a luddite at a technology fair. To overhear someone else's conversation was as dangerous as having the conversation yourself, and from the tone of the voices on the other side of Phillips' cubicle door, something was about to be said that he really didn't want to hear. With sudden resolve the Professor rose, hitched up his prison trousers, and marched confidently into the main body of the toilet.

He was met with four pairs of malevolent eyes, the scariest of which belong to the notorious Jock Fager.

"What the fuck are you doing in there?" Fager sneered in his thick Glaswegian accent.

"Just having a pee," said Phillips. He waved his hands in the air. "I haven't heard anything, I haven't seen anything, and I shall leave you fine gentlemen to whatever…" He looked from one accusatory pair of eyes to another, "… God bless!"

The Professor almost ran to the door.

"Oi, Professor!" Fager yelled after him. Phillips turned slowly, trying to hide his extreme fear.

"You keep your fucking mouth shut or I'll rip your fucking tongue out o' your fucking head!" Phillips nodded submissively. "Now fuck off!" concluded Fager.

Part Ten

The next day the Professor sat eagerly waiting for Julie at his usual table. He had all the paperwork ready for her arrival. Every other Wednesday was visitors' day, and today was that special day that had become the sole focus of each fortnight.

They only had a window of fifty minutes every two weeks, so every second counted. Julie arrived and went quickly to the table. Phillips thrust some papers at her.

"Right, I need you to look at..." Phillips began hastily without looking at her. His eyes scanned a notebook in front of him, "... pages seven, fifteen and thirty-five."

"And hello to you *also*, Professor," she said.

Phillips looked up.

"What? We don't have time to go through pleasantries at every visit. I asked you how you were two weeks ago. I really don't expect that much has change since then."

"Professor," Julie said forcefully, "we have two years to work on this. Even if you can function like a robot, I can't. I need a little human interaction now and again, all right?"

The Professor breathed deeply and tried to relax.

"I'm sorry, Julie. I've never been good at anything other than work. So, I focus on what I'm good at. I know I'm a pain, a cantankerous old pain in the arse, I know… You're right. You come all this way every two weeks and I just…"

"It's okay, Professor. Really, but I just need to talk a little… Sorry."

"What would you like to talk about?"

"I would really like to know how you're doing," Julie asked.

"I'm all right," said Phillips with a shrug.

"What are the *other* prisoners like?"

"I don't know. I don't have much to do with them…" The Professor cocked his head to one side and stared Julie in the eye. "I'm not an idiot, Julie. Is this *really* what you want to talk about?" Julie furrowed her brow, shook her head then looked away. "If you need to ask," continued the Professor, "for god's sake, just ask."

Julie sat down and studied the old man's face.

"Well, did you… do it?"

"You've sat there every other Wednesday for eight months," he said calmly. "Why have you never asked?"

"I don't know," Julie stammered. "Maybe I just don't want to hear…"

"… That your beloved Professor killed a man?" Julie shrugged and sighed. "If it helps, I didn't *kill* anyone," Phillips continued, then snorted a laugh through his nose. "I can't say there weren't times when

The Unforgiving Minute

I could have happily wrung the annoying bastard's neck." Julie turned away and involuntarily bit her lip. Phillips feared that in his attempt to handle the situation with a light touch, he had instead made things worse. "Julie, I'm sorry, really, I didn't mean to upset you… Look, he was a good man, really. As I say, he could be a pain at times, but can't we all… I mean look at how I'm messing this up right now. Julie, please look at me." She turned wet eyes to him. The level of her reaction confused him. "Did… did you know Alan Newton?" Julie instantly erupted into full-blown crying. The Professor took her hands. "Shit, sorry, I had no idea you knew him."

"I didn't know him," Julie said trying to control her crying.

"You didn't know him. Then why are you so upset?"

She shook her head, then laughed through the tears.

"I don't know… It just sort of hit me." Julie pulled a tissue from her pocket and dabbed at her eyes. "So what happened?"

"I… I don't know," Phillips sighed. "We were trying The Device for the first time. Alan thought we shouldn't go ahead with the experiment."

"Why?"

"Well, he was fearless when it came to theories, but…"

"But what?"

"I don't know," Phillips said bowing his head. "Maybe he was right. Maybe it *was* reckless to go ahead. Maybe it *was* too soon."

"Well, that was your decision," Julie said coldly, "and that one's on you." Phillips jerked his head up and stared at her. "We have to take responsibility for our actions, Professor. If you had something to do with Alan's death, then…"

"Julie," Phillips said slowly, "I didn't kill him, and I have no idea how he ended up buried in the woods."

Julie laughed tensely.

"Sorry… of course… sorry," she said, then smiled. "So, what *do* you remember?"

Phillips sat back and pushed some papers around on the table in front of him.

"When I regained consciousness, three hours had passed. I was amazed. The first attempt and I had travelled three hours into the future."

"And Alan?" Julie insisted.

"Alan wasn't there," Phillips said with gravitas, "I… I never saw him again."

"But," stammered Julie, "you must know something? People don't just vanish into thin air!"

"Julie, up until that moment people didn't time-travel either. This is a whole world of stuff we don't understand, but there are answers. Everything is knowable because everything is logical… cause and effect, Julie."

"But what if there are things we can't know? What if at the quantum scale, cause and effect have no meaning?"

"Really?" Phillips exclaimed, "we've been working together for eight months, and now I find out that you're another determinism denier."

The Unforgiving Minute

"I'm not denying anything," Julie insisted. "I just think it arrogant to be so certain in the face of uncertainty."

"And I think there are people who use that argument to avoid facing challenges that scare them."

"I don't deny that, Professor, but the universe is a very big place and we are very small. Responsible science leaves no room for hubris."

Phillips moved the papers around on the table, then glanced at his watch.

"Shall we get on? We only have twenty-five minutes left."

Part Eleven

James Boyce-Futch, the Governor of the prison, looked up as Phillips was marched into his office by a guard.

"Stop there!" instructed the guard.

Phillips halted in front of the Governor's desk.

"Professor?" said Boyce-Futch. He waited expectantly for a few moments. "You asked to see me."

"Yes…"

"Yes *Sir*, Phillips," barked the prison guard.

Boyce-Futch looked towards the guard and smiled pleasantly.

"Thank you, Clive. I'll call you when we're finished."

"Very well, Sir," the guard responded dutifully, then nodded stiffly and left the room.

"So Professor, what did you want to see me about?"

"I've been here eleven months now… Sir…" Phillips began.

"Mr. Boyce-Futch will do, Professor," the Governor interrupted gently.

"Well," said Phillips, "I've been continuing my research, as I'm sure you know, and… well… I need the

The Unforgiving Minute

machine I've been working on, to be able to move forwards. You see, I've done just about all I can do on paper. I really do need the actual machine."

"The *machine*?" Boyce-Futch repeated awkwardly. "Would this be the… erm…"

"Yes… the Time Machine," Phillips said with insincere levity, "yes Mr. Boyce-Futch, that machine."

"Well, that's a rather tall order, Professor. You see most of our inmates are busy making ceramic ashtrays or crafting wooden coat-hooks. Very few request permission to work on their… Time Machines."

"I do understand that it is a rather unusual request," said Phillips. "But I suppose I'm not the usual inmate."

"That you are not. What does this machine comprise of?"

"Oh, it's actually a very simple affair," explained the Professor. "A metal box with a run-of-of-the-mill electron gun…"

"*Gun!*" Boyce-Futch exclaimed.

"No, no," said Phillips waving his hands in the air, "an *electron* gun… a device for producing electrons, much like the ones used in the old glass tubed TV sets."

"Ah," said Boyce-Futch, "a cathode ray tube."

"I had no idea that you were scientific."

"I'm hardly an academic," said Boyce-Futch, "but people would do well to remember that I'm no bumbling idiot either."

"Who would think such a thing?" said Phillips flippantly.

Boyce-Futch stared at the Professor. His lips tight across his teeth.

"What else does this machine comprise of?"

"A standard particle detector that reads the spin of the electron, and a small needle. And that's it," concluded Phillips.

Boyce-Futch shook his head.

"Sorry, no, this is a prison, Phillips."

"But it really isn't anything dangerous or something that could cause any trouble," the Professor pleaded.

"Well, it did put you in here," said Boyce-Futch.

"With respect, a false accusation of murder put me in here."

"If you say so," said Boyce-Futch. He sat back in his chair. "Look Phillips, I'm not an unfair man. A good sort like you shouldn't really be in a place like this. I mean, there but for the grace of God, and all that. Look, if you keep your head down, play ball, maybe… just maybe, I may be able to do something."

"That would be wonderful, Sir," said Phillips. "I don't want to cause any trouble. In fact, if there is anything I can do… to help *you*?"

Boyce-Futch laughed, then cleared his throat.

"Well, Phillips, you may have noticed that this place is full of criminals?" The Professor nodded and smiled. "Having someone I can trust, someone that probably shouldn't really be here, on my side… keeping an eye on things… you get my drift."

"I do."

"Well, I may be able to bend a few rules for someone like that."

The Unforgiving Minute

Boyce-Futch nodded his head, then looked down at his desk. He pressed a red button on his phone.

"Yes, Sir," came a female voice from the loudspeaker.

"Send Clive in, will you, Joyce." Boyce-Futch looked up to Phillips. "So, we understand each other?"

"We do," said Phillips, simply.

The two men stared at each other in silence.

"You know that this may all be academic by next week?" said Boyce-Futch.

"Why?"

"You have an appointment with the parole board on Thursday."

"But… I've only done eleven months," said Phillips.

"It's standard practice with a conviction like yours; first parole hearing in month twelve. Don't get too excited, though. It usually comes to nothing… However… with a good word from the Governor…"

The guard appeared at the door.

"Come on, Phillips," ordered the guard.

The professor turned and walked towards the entrance.

"Professor?" called Boyce-Futch. Phillips looked back. "This machine of yours. Is it… real? I mean, does it really work?"

"If I could control time at will," answered Phillips, "do you think I'd be choosing to spend it in here?"

Part Twelve

During the winding route back to the cell block, Phillips found himself wringing every ounce of subtext from the conversation he had just had with the Governor. If he wanted to get his machine inside these walls, he was going to have to deliver something substantial.

By the time he had been marched back to the recreation area, an idea had blossomed in the rich soil of his imaginative brain. He stood and watched the warder, who had accompanied him, walk away with self-important but dubious purpose.

He scanned the room carefully until he found what he was looking for. Then he sat down, keeping an eye trained on a group of four prisoners that hovered threateningly in a secluded corner. Finally, the group started to move, and judging by their direction, the Professor's previous assumptions had been flawless. If he could get some usable information about this group's illegal operations, maybe that would be enough to gain favour with the Governor.

He stood up and followed the four men at a good distance. Phillips stopped at the end of a corridor and

The Unforgiving Minute

watched the group enter the lavatory. He casually leant against the wall. Over the next few minutes, he was joined by a number of other inmates who all assumed a position, either sitting or leaning, in the same overly self-conscious manner as had the Professor.

The door to the lavatory opened, and one of Jock Fager's minions poked his head into the hallway. He nodded to a small bald man, who immediately shuffled towards the toilet. He was inside a mere two minutes before re-emerging and scurrying away back towards the cell block.

Phillips watched this process repeat several times until he was the only one left. The head appeared at the toilet door again and looked up and down the corridor. His gaze fell on Phillips. The man stared, then narrowed his eyes. If Phillips was going to do this, he needed to do it now. The Professor started to walk slowly towards the man.

"What do you want?" the man said aggressively as Phillips reached him.

"The same as everyone else,"

"You?" the man laughed.

"Why not?" said the Professor. "I'm human. Stuck in here like everybody else."

The man looked Phillips up and down.

"Fuck off!" he said simply.

"I want to see Fager."

"Well, 'e don't want to see no *nonce*."

"I'm not a *nonce*," said the Professor indignantly, "I'm a murderer!"

"I thought you was innocent?" sneered the man.

The Professor smiled.

"Aren't we all?"

The man looked amused by Phillips comment, but his mouth refused to smile. He shot a furtive glance up and down the corridor, then waved a hand.

"Well, come on then, *nonce*," he said. "We 'aven't got all fucking day."

Phillips followed the man into the drab and ill-fragranced room. Fager watched them approach. As the Professor neared him, he took an aggressive step forwards.

"What the fuck do you want, ya fucking *nonce*?"

"The *nonce* says 'e's a murderer not a *nonce*," said the man leading Phillips.

The professor graciously bowed his head.

"I'd like to buy some… stuff."

"Oh, you would, would ya," Fager taunted. "And what stuff would this be?"

"I… crr… I don't know," stammered Phillips. "What do you have?"

"What do I have?" Fager mocked, imitating Phillips' Oxbridge accent. He turned to one of the other prisoners. "Well, don't stand around. Show the Prof a menu."

Phillips was shocked. He believed Fager to be wily, but wasn't expecting such a level of organisation. Phillips looked expectantly at Fager. Fager suddenly exploded in a rage that the Professor had only ever seen in films.

"Are you a fucking madman as well as a *nonce*?" Fager yelled centimetres from Phillips face. "You

The Unforgiving Minute

actually think we have a fucking menu?" He punched Phillips in the eye. The Professor tripped and fell heavily to the floor. "I told ya what I'd do to you, didn't I?"

"Yes, you did," said the Professor nursing his face and cowering.

Phillips was fully expecting to be beaten to death, but as seconds passed, the attack failed to come. He looked up at Fager and noticed that the big Scot had unzipped his flies and was in the process of rummaging beneath his trousers. Fager extracted his penis from the aperture. Tufts of bright red hair protruded from around the man's phallus. Fager held himself with his right hand and began to urinate onto the Professor. The hot torrent seemed endless and had a putrid aroma from the asparagus that had been served for lunch. But the absolute humiliation of this act was totally overshadowed by the incomprehensible silence in which it was carried out. When Fager had squeezed out every last drop, he tucked himself back into his trousers and pulled up his zip. The four men then left, still in complete silence leaving the Professor and his ill-conceived plan on the filthy lavatory floor.

Part Thirteen

The heavy metal clunk of the cell door mechanism unlocking woke Phillips just moments before the ear-piercing siren completed the prison wake-up call. He climbed out of bed and went over to the washbasin. He stared at himself in the wall mirror. Not much of the silvered rectangle remained functional. Years of water damage had covered the mirror with black and grey splodges necessitating the need to bob one's head around in order to view the whole of one's face. Phillips inspected his black eye. He had hoped that by today it would have faded as the parole board would probably not think a shiner the most convincing indicator of a rehabilitated man.

Phillips lined up outside his cell, and three prison guards herded the fifteen men in Section C towards the showers. Once all of Section C had vacated the wash block, they were led single-file back to their cells. They had ten minutes to change into their day clothes and be back outside their cells ready to be taken to the dining hall for breakfast. Life in a prison was a never ending procession of depressing congas.

The Unforgiving Minute

When Phillips got back to his cell he found the suit with which he had entered the prison had been neatly placed on his bunk. After breakfast, the Professor was escorted to the admin block that was, at all other times, off limits to prisoners. He waited in the corridor until a kindly looking woman emerged from an office and beckoned him in. Phillips was invited to sit down in front of a panel of two women and two men who were seated behind a long desk.

"So," said a late middle-aged man whom Phillips took to be in charge, "you are Edward Vivian Phillips?" The Professor nodded. "So, how are things going?"

"All right," Phillips responded, nodding enthusiastically.

"Any problems?" the man continued momentarily peering down at some notes.

"No, everything's… okay."

The second man breathed loudly, making his presence known.

"I suppose you walked into something, did you?" asked the second man. Phillips shook his head. "How'd you get that black eye, then?"

"I know you probably see a lot of people in this job that simply tell you a pack of lies," said Phillips. "I'm a scientist. I have spent my whole life in pursuit of the truth. I can assure you that that is all you'll hear from me today."

"So," asked the kindly woman gently, "how did you get a black eye?"

"I was punched."

Paul Casselle

"I'm so sorry," said the woman. "Have you reported it?"

"Forgive me," said Phillips, "you have all probably seen a lot more of prison life than I have, but you have not seen it from this side. The law exists only in the world of the innocent. Justice stops at the point of conviction."

"Are you saying that there is no place for justice in here?" asked the woman.

"Oh no," answered the Professor, "there's definitely a place for it, just no room." He laughed, then leant forwards conspiratorially, "You may have noticed, this prison is crawling with criminals."

The four parole panellists made a show of resisting levity.

"Do you think this is funny?" said the woman with a sharpness designed to wound rather than be witty.

"No," responded Phillips shaking his head, "if you good people spent one day behind bars, you'd realise that as much as law-abiding society likes to think that criminals can be rehabilitated given enough care and understanding, it's a lie. A lie with which we try to protect our terrified socialist selves. But just as ignorance of the law is no defence, neither is ignorance of the truth. And the truth is that even though this low-security prison is seen as the palatable face of punishment, it is most definitely not. It's a fucking hell hole!"

The man that seemed to be in charge shifted superiorly in his chair.

The Unforgiving Minute

"I really don't think there is any need for that kind of language," he said.

"And that's my point," said Phillips, "you wouldn't, would you, sitting that side of the desk."

"What is that supposed to mean?" interjected the woman, hiding injury behind indignance.

"You, my good lady, do not have a black eye," said Phillips plainly, "and I am sure you have never suffered the humiliation of having a rather large Scot empty his bladder onto you while you lay on the floor reeling from his well placed right-hander."

Part Fourteen

"That, Professor," said Boyce-Futch, "is not the way to behave at a bloody parole hearing." His face betrayed incandescent rage although his professionalism was managing to contain it. "If you don't want me to just wash my hands of you and throw you to the lions, you'll learn how to control yourself and do as you're told."

"You're right, Sir. I won't even begin to defend myself. I don't think I've ever lost it to that degree before… except, maybe with my wife."

"Well, I'm at least glad that you're not going to try and justify that abomination. I don't suppose I need to tell you that they stamped your file 'rejected' before you had made it back to your cell?" Phillips nodded his head. "Are you willing to at least try and do some good?"

"Yes, Mr Boyce-Futch."

"Good," said the Governor calming down and descending into the chair behind his desk, "I need you to do something for me… A delicate matter."

"Okay," responded the Professor, intrigued.

Boyce-Futch looked towards the open door of his office, then back to Phillips.

The Unforgiving Minute

"Shut the door," said Boyce-Futch in little more than a whisper. Phillips crossed to the door and closed it. "Come and sit down." Phillips sat and frowned. "Sorry, I'm just not sure who I can trust." He paused. "The Home Office is on my back again about stamping out incidences of illegal drugs possession within the prison."

"A rather tall order," said Phillips.

"I believe," continued Boyce-Futch, "that there is a single man controlling the whole thing."

"I can tell you who that is, Sir," said Phillips. Boyce-Futch stared at him. "Jock Fager."

"I know it's bloody Jock Fager!" Boyce-Futch shouted, then immediately reduced his volume. "I know it's Jock Fager. I know that already. I just need to prove it."

"How do you do that?"

"I need to catch him bang to rights. Then I can get him transferred out of here. Let him be someone else's problem."

"And I can help?"

"Yes you can. I need someone to set up a deal with him, then tip me off so we can catch him red-handed." Phillips exhaled loudly. "I know, I know, I'm asking a lot… but so are you… bloody… Time… Machine…"

"How would this work?" asked Phillips.

"Do you know Fager?"

"Oh yes, I know Fager."

Boyce-Futch narrowed his eyes and cocked his head questioningly.

"You… you don't do drugs yourself, do you?"

Paul Casselle

"No, don't be silly, Sir," said Phillips. "Reality's difficult enough without messing with my brain as well!"

"Quite. Listen. I'll give you the money to tempt Fager to make a deal. You just set it up and tip me off." Phillips stared at the Governor and nervously licked his lips. "You want your bloody machine, right?" Phillips nodded. "Then do this."

Boyce-Futch unlocked a drawer in his desk and placed a bulging manila envelope in front of the Professor.

"That's the money," said the Governor.

"How much is there?"

"Three thousand."

"Pounds?"

"Yes. Three thousand pounds."

"And I'll get my machine?"

"Yes."

Phillips moved to pick up thc cnvelope, but Boyce-Futch stopped him with a strong hand.

"Do you actually think I'm going to let you walk out of here with three thousand pounds in cash?" said the Governor. "No Professor, just set the deal up and let me know when and where."

"And I just don't turn up?"

"No, you have to go or Fager will know something's up and we won't catch him in the act."

"Hold on, let me get this right," said the Professor. "You want me to go to a drugs deal with Fager *without* the money?"

The Unforgiving Minute

"No. Listen. When you're ready to do the deal, Clive - Officer Connelly - will hand you the money, okay?"

"Officer Connelly knows?"

Boyce-Futch nodded.

"You can't tell anyone about this, you understand? There are only two… now three people who know about it," explained the Governor. "As I said, I think some of my staff may be involved with Fager, but I'll deal with *that* later. For now, I want Fager out of here. So, do the deal and tell Officer Connelly where and when. Before you meet with Fager, Connelly will give you the money."

Phillips knocked tentatively on the open cell door. Fager looked up from lying on his bunk. He started to get up.

"I'm going to fucking kill you, you fucking…"

"Three thousand pounds," said Phillips.

"What?"

"I want to buy some coke. Three thousand pounds."

"You don't do drugs, you *nonce*," countered Fager.

"But I *do* have three thousand."

"Cash?" Phillips nodded. "Where'd you get three grand?"

"That doesn't matter. What matters is, can you handle that much?"

"Don't you worry about me, Prof… You want coke?"

"Three thousand pounds' worth, yes."

"Okay, Prof. Tomorrow, after lunch, usual place."

"I'll see you then," Phillips said turning to go.

"Hey, Prof," Fager called after him. Phillips looked at the big Scot. "If yous are fucking me around, I will fucking kill ya. You know that, right?"

"I have no doubt, Mr Fager. No doubt at all."

Part Fifteen

Phillips' appetite had deserted him. He was so nervous at lunch that he couldn't even face the carton of orange juice that sat on the metal tray next to his untouched meal.

On the other side of the dining hall, he saw Fager and his entourage get up and head out of the room. Phillips waited a moment, then pushed his chair away from the table. He felt weak, possibly because he had not eaten a thing since breakfast, but more likely because he felt more terrified than he had ever felt in his life.

As he walked down the corridor towards the lavatory, he could see Officer Connelly hiding in an alcove on the other side of the lavatory door. Phillips walked the last few metres and looked expectantly towards Connelly. The Officer nodded, then ducked out of sight as the door was suddenly opened by one of Fager's men.

"Come on then, *nonce*." said Fager's man.

"I'll be right there," said Phillips. The man stared at the Professor. "I said I'll be right there. If you want to mess this deal up for Fager, just keep fucking around. I'm sure he will have no trouble showing his gratitude for doing him out of three thousand pounds." The man opened his mouth and hesitated. "Go inside," Phillips said as if talking to a toddler, "and tell your boss that I'm just coming. Go on, run along."

The man went into the toilet, and Phillips pulled the door closed.

"Officer Connelly," he whispered. The Officer's head appeared. "Can I have the money?"

Connelly narrowed his eyes.

"First," whispered Connelly, "go inside and make sure Fager has the stuff. Then come back out here and I'll give you the money and radio the Governor and the other officers."

"But why can't I just take the money now," asked the Professor. "Fager's not going to be able to get away."

"This is not my first time carrying out a sting, Professor. Do it my way and everything will go just as we want it."

Phillips hesitated, then drew a large breath and pushed the door open. Fager was leaning against a washbasin. He silently watched Phillips approach.

"Have you got the money?" asked Fager.

"Do you have the drugs?" responded Phillips.

"Don't fuck me around, *nonce*."

"Look, Mr Fager, you *show* me that you have the drugs and *I'll* give you your money. Someone is holding it for me just outside the door."

"Are yous saying you don't trust me?" said Fager. "Because *that* would hurt my feelings."

The Unforgiving Minute

"It's not a question of trust, Mr Fager. It's a question of prudent negotiation."

Fager looked around his entourage.

"You see, boys, isn't it nice to do business with such a cultured and intelligent man." He turned to Phillips. "And such a trustworthy one as well, eh?" Fager stared threateningly into the Professor's eyes, then turned and signalled one of his men. The man brought a backpack over to Fager. The Scot unzipped the main compartment and showed Phillips several neatly wrapped bags of white powder that were within. "Them is the drugs, Professor. Now give me my money."

Phillips struggled not to smile as he backed up, turned, then walked quickly towards the lavatory door. This had actually been much easier than he had imagined. Phillips reached the door and pulled it open. He stepped through into the corridor, then urgently looked left and right. The corridor was empty. Connelly was gone.

"Where's my fucking money, *nonce*?" came Fager's voice in a whisper centimetres from the Professor's ear.

Part Sixteen

Julie had had a lot of trouble finding a parking space in central London, but as she turned the same corner she had already been around seven times, she spotted a blue Lexus pulling away from a parking meter. At least something was going her way this afternoon. The space she had managed to grab was only a short walk from the place she was visiting.

For most of the previous year, Julie had wanted to make this visit, but fear of what she might find out had stopped her. Knowledge cannot be undone, and the chronic pain of the unknown had been easier to bear than the wounds she believed the truth might inflict upon her.

Julie climbed the stairs to the impressive building and quickly found her way to the Chief Court Clerk's office. She knocked and heard a voice inside instruct her to come in. Seated at an ancient dark oak desk was a suited man in his early thirties. She caught him half way between sitting down to his lunch, and rising to greet her.

"Hello," she said pleasantly, "I'm Julie Taggart."

The Unforgiving Minute

"Very pleased to meet you. Please excuse me eating my lunch," the man said with a laugh, then extended a welcoming hand. "So, how can I help you?"

"I'm a friend of Professor Edward Phillips."

"So you said on the phone."

"I was wondering if you could fill in some blank spaces from the day of his trial?"

"What do you mean, 'blank spaces'? Sorry, Miss Taggart, I don't follow."

"Well, his lawyer Mr Smythe told me that he managed to get an unusual request of the Professor's granted."

"And what was that?" said the clerk with a fleeting, but plainly evident glance at the uneaten sandwich on his desk.

"Please," Julie said, "please don't let me stop you from having your lunch."

"Thank you, Miss Taggart," he said picking up a tuna and cress sandwich. "What was this unusual request?"

He held out his lunch plate to Julie.

"Thank you," she said with a polite wave of her hand, "I've already had lunch."

Julie smiled.

"The unusual request?" prompted the clerk.

"Yes. You remember that he claimed that he didn't commit the... murder because he was... err... time-traveling?"

"Yes, Miss Taggart, I do."

"Well, apparently, according to his lawyer, he asked for his time-machine when he was in the cells here. Just after he was sentenced."

"No," the clerk said with a shake of his head. "I can't see that happening. I'm sorry, Miss Taggart, but the lawyer must be wrong. We definitely would not let a convicted man have a piece of suspect machinery in his cell." His face became set and pompous. "Especially such a contentious device."

"Well, that's what I thought, but Mr Smythe was quite sure that it *did* happen."

The clerk rose from his desk and went to a filing cabinet. He slid out drawers in turn until he found what he was looking for and returned to his desk. He held up the ledger he had retrieved.

"You've got me very curious, Miss Taggart. I want to see who was on detention duty that day. Ah," he said, consulting the ledger, "Charlie." He looked up. "I can't see any way Charlie would allow such a thing."

"I'm really sorry to be such a bother, but is there any way we could… check with him?"

The clerk was ahead of her and had already picked up his phone and dialled a number. He held up his hand, indicating for Julie to wait.

"Hello," he said into the phone, "is Charlie in today? Ah, right, excellent… Is he on duty by himself?… No… Perfect. Then would you please tell him to come straight to my office… Thank you." He looked at Julie. "Well, hopefully he'll be able to confirm that there was no way Professor Phillips could have had his machine in the cells."

The Unforgiving Minute

Five minutes later, there was a knock at the clerk's door, and a late middle-aged uniformed man entered.

"You wanted to see me, Sir," said Charlie.

"Yes, this is Miss Taggart. She's inquiring about the detention of Professor Edward Phillips."

"Yes Sir, I was on duty that day."

"Apparently, the Professor's lawyer claims that he was allowed to have his… device in the cell with him?" explained the clerk. Charlie went very quiet and chewed his lip. "That didn't happen, did it Charlie?"

"Well… Sir… it was a very unusual day. The place was teeming with reporters and the poor old Professor seemed to sort of… lose his marbles a bit, Sir… And I was all by myself."

"Charlie, are you saying that you *did* let him have this device in his cell?"

"Well it was a very small device… I couldn't see what harm it would do."

The clerk turned to Julie.

"Well, it seems I owe Mr Smythe an apology."

"What happened to The Device after the Professor was taken to prison?" asked Julie.

"I locked it in the evidence room, Miss," responded Charlie.

"Will it still be there?"

"I don't see why not."

Julie turned to the clerk.

"Is there any chance I could see it?"

"If it's there, I don't see any reason why not," said the clerk. "I mean, it's not evidence, is it?"

Charlie led Julie into the bowels of the courthouse where the evidence room was situated. After a couple of minutes rummaging, Charlie presented Julie with the small black box. Julie examined it carefully.

"So this is the famous Time Machine?" Julie said.

"Not as impressive as H. G. Wells', but yes, Miss."

"This display on the top," Julie asked pointing to the date and time indicator on the upper face of the device. "Is this as it was left by the Professor?"

"I'm pretty certain it is."

"You see," Julie indicated the display, "these numbers… they haven't been moved since the Professor was here?"

"As I said, Miss, I'm pretty sure this is how he left it."

"Excellent, Charlie… I don't suppose… I could take the machine?"

Charlie grabbed the black box from her.

"No, Miss. This is staying locked in here. It's caused me enough grief for one day, thank you very much!"

"Of course, of course," Julie said sympathetically. "May I just jot down the date and time from the display, though?"

"If you're quick, Miss. I need to be getting back to work."

Julie wrote the data in a small notebook, then Charlie locked the machine away.

"Thank you for your help, Charlie," she said as she turned to go.

The Unforgiving Minute

On her way back to her car, her mobile rang. She pulled it from her pocket and placed it against her ear.

"Hello?"

"Hello, Julie Taggart?"

"Speaking."

"I'm calling from the prison about Professor Phillips."

"Yes…"

"I'm afraid I have some very bad news. Are you a relative?"

"Just a friend. What sort of bad news?"

"I'm afraid… I'm really so sorry… Professor Phillips… passed away this afternoon.

Part Seventeen

"We didn't know who else to call, Miss Taggart," said Boyce-Futch. "The professor's wife is deceased and he has no other relatives, so… I thought of you."

"No, that's all right," said Julie, "I'm glad you called me." There was a long awkward pause. "What… what happened, exactly?"

"At the moment… we're not absolutely sure, but it seems to have been a dispute between the Professor and another inmate that got out of hand."

"A dispute? What sort of dispute?"

"People in here can act very out of character, Miss Taggart. As much as we try to run a clean ship, it's not the most comfortable of places. Tempers get frayed, people get desperate. They do things that they'd never do on the outside…"

"Please, can you just tell me straight," Julie interrupted with some passion. "The man is dead, and you don't seem to be taking this very seriously."

"Miss Taggart, I assure you that we take prison deaths *extremely* seriously, and we are doing everything we can to get to the bottom of this. But you must understand, some of the inmates really don't help themselves."

"What exactly are you accusing the Professor of doing?"

"As I said, Miss Taggart, people on the inside can do things that are very out of character."

"So," insisted Julie, exasperation turning to anger, "what did he do?"

"He seemed to have developed a... drug habit," said Boyce-Futch.

"A what!?"

"As I've been trying to tell you, very out of character for someone like the Professor, but I have seen it before. Some just find the pressure of incarceration simply too much."

"You are seriously claiming that the Professor had a drug habit?"

"The man that has been arrested for his murder is a notorious drugs dealer. He's now been taken to a maximum-security prison. I've wanted him out of here for a long time, but until now we couldn't find enough proof."

"So the Professor did you a favour. Is that what you are saying?"

"No," Boyce-Futch pleaded, "no, believe me, we are all very shocked and saddened by what happened. I'm just saying that at least the culprit is in a place where he can do no further harm."

"Or give you further headaches," Julie concluded.

Boyce-Futch sighed deeply and moved his gaze to a large cardboard box on his desk.

Paul Casselle

"We weren't sure what to do with all his papers," he said. "Normally we give the personal belongings to the next of kin, or if there isn't one, simply burn the effects. The Professor's stuff seemed too important to just incinerate. We thought you might like to have it."

Julie rummaged through the box.

"Thank you, for not just destroying it all," she said. "Is there anything else?"

"Well, yes," said Boyce-Futch, "his burial. What would you like to do?"

"Me?" said Julie. "He was killed on your watch. I think that's your responsibility not mine."

"But I thought…"

Julie interrupted Boyce-Futch.

"I was just someone that was working with him on his research. He was not a friend. We just worked together." Boyce-Futch's mouth gaped a little. "Is there anything else?" she repeated.

"No," said Boyce-Futch. "You just need to sign for his belongings." He pointed to a form on his desk. "If I could just have your signature here."

Boyce-Futch offered Julie a pen. She signed quickly, then picked up the cardboard box.

"Thank you," she said as she turned to go.

"Erm… sorry," said Boyce-Futch.

Julie turned and looked blankly at him. Boyce-Futch was holding the form Julie had just signed. She shook her head questioningly.

"Is there a problem?" she asked.

"You've signed 'Julie Newton'," said Boyce-Futch, "I thought your name was Taggart?"

The Unforgiving Minute

"Oh, did I sign Newton? I usually go by my maiden name, Taggart. I wasn't thinking. Newton's my married name. Do you need me to sign again?"

"No, that's fine," said Boyce-Futch. Julie turned to go. "It's just that?…" She stopped and looked quizzically at Boyce-Futch. "Your married name's 'Newton'?" Julie nodded. "Wasn't that the name of the man that the Professor was accused of killing, Alan Newton?" Julie stared silently. "Is that just a coincidence?"

"I… err," Julie stammered.

"Are you the widow of Alan Newton?" Boyce-Futch asked plainly.

Julie swallowed hard and her eyes began to water.

"Yes," she said, "yes, I am."

Part Eighteen

Two years later

Julie Taggart stood at the front of a lecture theatre at Trinity College, Cambridge. She looked at the eager-eyed first year physics undergraduates.

"The main thing you need to understand," said Julie, "is that whatever you have experienced in your life up to now will be of absolutely no help at all in your understanding of quantum physics. As Richard Feynman once said, 'If you think you understand quantum mechanics, you don't understand quantum mechanics'. Don't look for answers that you, at the scale in which we all live, can understand. Simply concentrate on what fits.

The laws that govern the infinitesimally small appear to be so radically different from the classical laws that govern all that we see with our naked eyes that it would be madness to try to understand. To work in this field you must abandon understanding and embrace acceptance. In the subatomic realm, the impossible is normal." She paused and looked around the room at the

The Unforgiving Minute

terrified faces. "If I've managed to scare you half to death, I've achieved fifty percent of my work in teaching you about quantum physics." A bell started ringing. "Go on, go and have some lunch."

Julie walked to her office and sat down at her desk. She stared at the clock on the wall. It had a large analogue face that read almost exactly one o'clock, and next to it, a date display. She stared unblinkingly at the date for which she had been waiting for six months. The enormity of the event that she believed would occur today might prove to be both a revelatory vindication of her scientific theories, but also a challenge to her deepest held morals.

After the Professor's death two years ago, she had continued to study his theories as well as becoming totally familiar with the work of her late husband. Six months ago she had had a *eureka* moment that had left her so dazzled by its conclusions that she had called in sick and found it impossible to return to work for a whole week.

The Professor's device really did work. It caused, via apparent quantum uncertainty, the splitting into two of an infinity of universes. The outcome of which meant that the operator would either travel forward in time or would not, depending on which side of the split one ended up.

But the Professor had reported time and time again an anomaly that he couldn't understand; what he described as a strange memory aberration that came with each use of The Device. In one instance, he would jump a period of time and on returning, hear reports of what he did while he was jumping, but he would have no memory of the period. However, on occasions the jump would not work. He would go through the event he was trying to avoid, but find that although he had full recollection of the events he had just lived through, everyone involved had no memory of him being present at all.

The revelation Julie had had six months ago was based on something she had suspected from the very beginning. When the device operator used the machine, they would either jump into a parallel universe at a future time or jump into a parallel universe remaining at the present time. But the particles that made up the actual body of the operator in both universes became quantumly entangled, and when the operator that hadn't jumped forward in time reached the future time set on the device, the two identical operators returned to their own universes, but retained all the memories of their experiences during the universe exchange.

This in itself was beyond extraordinary, but the consequences of this took eighteen months to coalesce in Julie's brain. After being sentenced to three years in prison, the Professor had tried to use The Device to jump the whole three years, but unluckily he was the operator that jumped to a parallel universe, but at the same time; he didn't jump forwards.

Julie glanced at the clock again. Today was the date the Professor had set on the device to jump his prison sentence. Today at five o'clock the two Professors would swap back to their own original universes. But the Professor in the universe that Julie lived in was dead

The Unforgiving Minute

and had been buried in a Cambridge cemetery two years ago. If Julie was correct, at five o'clock today the living Professor in the other universe would swap places with the rotting corpse in this one.

It was four o'clock when Julie parked her car in the cemetery carpark. She opened the boot and retrieved a spade and a stethoscope, then went in search of the Professor's grave.

It took her a little while to remember the location of the Professor's burial site from when she had attended his funeral two years ago. Now, she stood over his neglected gravestone with her spade in one hand and her stethoscope in the other. She glanced at her watch; it was ten past four. If she was right, the living Professor would materialise in fifty minutes six feet beneath where she stood.

She looked around. It was a Wednesday afternoon and the graveyard was totally empty. No one would witness her actions, and that is exactly as she wanted it. She looked at her watch repeatedly, confused by the emotions she was feeling. Part of her was impatient for five o'clock to arrive, while another part of her was terrified by what that may bring.

She turned her wrist to look at her watch for the umpteenth time just as the minute hand slid silently onto the number twelve. She fell to her knees dropping the spade to one side. Julie placed the eartips of the stethoscope into her ears and the listening drum to the earth of the Professor's grave. She held her breath and tremored with fear.

There! She was sure she had heard something. A slight movement, a quantum shift beneath the soil. She doubled her efforts to steady her breathing. The noise was unmistakable, repeating and growing in intensity. There was no doubt in her mind. She listened again, her face distorting with every emotion she had ever felt, but all at the same time; tearing her apart. Scratch, scratch, scratch. Although she tried not to, the image of the Professor suddenly appearing in that cold dark coffin below her feet made vomit rise in her throat.

Six hours maximum. That's what her research had suggested. A person buried six feet down in a standard coffin could stay alive for up to six hours before suffocating. The calculation had been made to take into account the accelerated use of available oxygen due to extreme panic.

But this was the man that had caused the premature death of her husband, and she had an opportunity to kill him in retribution; an eye for an eye; a death for a death. But more than that, she could enact the perfect murder. If she did nothing, the Professor would surely die by her hand, yet no one would be able to convict her of anything. And yet, the man about to die a horrible painful death beneath her feet was one of the most brilliant minds she had ever known. For god's sake! He had invented time-travel and proved the many-worlds hypothesis.

Julie had waited six months for this moment, but now it was here, every resolve she had made deserted her. Minutes ticked by. She listened time and time again and heard the same; desperate scratching and muffled

The Unforgiving Minute

cries. She sat back against the gravestone and rocked backwards and forwards like a committed lunatic in an insane asylum, her face awash with tears.

She suddenly became aware that the daylight had gone. In confused panic she stared at her watch. It was ten o'clock. 'Where had the time gone?' she thought. She threw herself, prostrate onto the soil and listened with the stethoscope; nothing. Everything was silent. She checked her watch again.

"This isn't right!" she screamed. "He still has another hour!"

Grabbing the spade she started to dig desperately, having finally made the impossible choice; to save the life of her husband's murderer. Unless of course, she had left it too late.

…-…

If you enjoyed ***The Unforgiving Minute***, please take a moment to leave a review on Amazon. It means so much to me to hear that readers liked my books. Also, more reviews helps immensely with my visibility on Amazon, and other readers might find ***The Unforgiving Minute***.

So, please take a moment, and let me know what you think.

Bedfellows Thriller Series
By Paul Casselle

If The Bed Falls In
A psychological thriller that shines a spotlight on the shady dealings that may be the true reason so much is going wrong in our society.

Guerrillas by Night
A companion novella to the Bedfellows series. It tells the story of Book One from a fascinating new perspective. It follows the backstory of a very enigmatic female character from the pages of *If The Bed Falls In*.

As Mad as Hell

This second book in the series, takes us so much deeper as we follow a rogue MI6 agent using every resource he can to hunt down the culprits behind the *New World Order*. But he is a man battling with his own internal demons as well as the One Percenters.

Other books by Paul Casselle

Conversations with Eric

Full of mystery, painfully funny situations and twisting plots, Simon picks his way through an ever thickening soup of intrigue and murder. At every turn, he tries to get out, but he continues to be sucked in by murderous villains and the psychologically damaged criminal class.

Everyone Else's Everyone Else (Short Story)

From morning to sundown, the machinations of London's humanity ebb and flow, intermingling with each other in the way only we happily, insane humans can.
We all have our stories, but to a stranger on the street...who are we, and who are they?

New World Order? No Way Out? (Non-Fiction)
Many of us are becoming aware of a growing global problem with national economies and terrorism, but some believe we are being led down this path by powerful people determined to destroy our free society in favour of their own greed. So, is this conspiracy nonsense?

Blue Skies over Dark Days (An unreliable memoir)
These are true tales - well, mostly. In this first volume of autobiographical episodes, I have allowed a little artistic licence to hopefully turn some extraordinary events from my life into funny and often moving pieces.

Printed in Great Britain
by Amazon